DOUBLE OR
NOTHING

DOUBLE OR NOTHING

Brooke Carter

orca soundings

ORCA BOOK PUBLISHERS

Published in Canada and the United States in 2020 by Orca Book Publishers.
orcabook.com

Library and Archives Canada Cataloguing in Publication
Title: Double or nothing / Brooke Carter.
Names: Carter, Brooke, 1977– author.
Series: Orca soundings.
Description: Series statement: Orca soundings
Identifiers: Canadiana (print) 20200176099 | Canadiana (ebook) 20200176102 |
ISBN 9781459823815 (softcover) | ISBN 9781459823822 (PDF) |
ISBN 9781459823839 (EPUB)
Classification: LCC PS8605.A77776 D68 2020 | DDC jc813/.6—dc23

Library of Congress Control Number: 2020930588

Summary: In this high-interest accessible novel for teen readers,
when a teenage genius descends deeper into a gambling addiction,
her twin sister becomes embroiled in her dangerous game.

Orca Book Publishers is committed to reducing the consumption
of nonrenewable resources in the making of our books. We make
every effort to use materials that support a sustainable future.

Orca Book Publishers gratefully acknowledges the support for its
publishing programs provided by the following agencies: the Government
of Canada, the Canada Council for the Arts and the Province of British
Columbia through the BC Arts Council and the Book Publishing Tax Credit.

Edited by Tanya Trafford
Design by Ella Collier
Cover images by Gettyimages.ca/Asia Marosa / EyeEm and
Shutterstock.com/Krasovski Dmitri (back)

Printed and bound in Canada.

23 22 21 20 • 1 2 3 4

For my parents,

and for second chances.

Chapter One

I turn my lucky coin over in my fingers, slipping the cool metal from one knuckle to another. I flip it and wonder, Will it be heads? Or tails? I'm amazed by the odds. Not just the odds of my own coin flips, but the odds of everything. Of the weird connections between people and events. Of winning or losing my favorite game, poker. Or the odds I'm thinking of right now as I sit in a third-year English class watching a movie about *Hamlet*.

I'm only in this class because I need it for my early entrance scholarship. Most people don't go to college when they're fifteen, like I did. They most certainly don't take advanced courses like I do now at the ripe old age of eighteen. This class so boring (I'm pre-med, and I prefer math), but the movie we're watching has some redeeming qualities. *Rosencrantz & Guildenstern Are Dead* is about a couple of nobodies whose job it is to watch over the nutcase Hamlet.

It's kind of blowing my mind right now, because the characters are talking about the odds of coin flips, and Guildenstern's coin is coming up heads every time. Right when I just happen to be fiddling with my own lucky coin. It's a 1970 American quarter. My grandpa gave it to me before he died. He was really into coin collecting. The cool thing is that it's a special sample of a coin, called a proof. It was cast on top of a 1941 Canadian quarter by accident. Grandpa told me that no one knows how the Canadian coin got mixed up in the US mint, but it's pretty neat. Apparently there are a lot of them in circulation.

I'm supposed to be thinking about the themes in this movie, but as usual I'm thinking a thousand things at once. I'm thinking about the coin combinations on the screen. I'm thinking about probability theory. I'm thinking about the odds of my coin matching the flips the characters make. I'm thinking about Hamlet and the sucky life he's living. To be or not to be, dude. Yeah, that is the question.

I'm thinking about how I will pass this course. I'm thinking about my twin sister, Aggie. She's also a genius and is sitting next to me. She is enjoying this movie in a way I never could. This is the only class we share together, and that's a good thing. I hate having Aggie always checking up on me.

But mostly I'm thinking about my cell phone. The prof made me turn it off when I got to class. But I had several windows open. Online gambling and stock-trading apps. Every second that goes by, I'm losing money.

Aggie thinks we're not rooming together this year because I need space to figure out who I am besides a twin. But really it's so that I can gamble in privacy. I count cards, analyze stats, make bets. Flip coins. Normal teen-genius-gambling-addict stuff.

Our English prof, a hairy, young Mark Ruffalo-type named Dr. Dave Murray, stops the movie.

"We'll watch the rest tomorrow," he says. "In the meantime I want you to think about tragic flaws..."

I start tuning him out and gathering my stuff together. "Whatever, Dr. Dave," I mutter.

Aggie gives me a side-eye. "Shh."

"Think about Hamlet's tragic flaw in particular," Dr. Dave continues. "Anyone care to tell us what it is?" He scans the room, waiting. "Come on, you've all read the play."

His gaze lands on me. "Ester Tomasi," he says. "You seem ready to share." He challenges me with a look.

I sigh. "He's unlucky," I say, and Dr. Dave looks surprised.

"Care to elaborate?" he asks.

"Well, look what happens to him. His dad dies, probably murdered by his own mother and uncle, then his dead dad haunts him and asks him to seek revenge. He can't trust anyone. His girlfriend kills herself. He pretty much loses his mind. And then he dies in the end! I mean, the odds of all these things happening, not to mention all the cases of mistaken identity and double-crossings, are astronomical. I'd call that pretty unlucky."

Dr. Dave nods slowly. "Anyone have a different take?" he asks. "Agatha?"

He looks at my sister, who shifts uncomfortably in the seat next to me. I know she hates this as much as I do. Not the class, but the constant competition people force us into. It's like we can't exist without being compared to the other. It's Twin Torture™.

I stare at her, and she falters a bit as she speaks.

"Um, I had a slightly different take," she begins.

Oh, Aggie, ever the diplomatic one.

"Go on," says Dr. Dave.

"I think Hamlet's tragic flaw is that he can't make decisions."

Dr. Dave nods, and I can see that Aggie's going to get yet another gold star for this one.

She continues. "Hamlet is really smart, but he overthinks everything to the point that he can't act. And that makes everything fall apart for him." She glances at me. I can tell she feels bad for me.

For some reason that bugs me. My points are just as valid. "If it's not about luck and odds," I say, "then why did this movie starring characters from *Hamlet* open with coin flips? And why have we been talking about this so-called Wheel of Fortune all semester?"

"Well, that's not really—" Dr. Dave starts, but I keep talking.

"No, the whole thing is completely absurd. Do you know what the odds are of getting heads ninety-two times in a row? It's, like, one in two, but to the hundredth power. So, to me, that's saying it's just down to fate. And if that's the case, then what hope do any of us have? There's no free will. Just the indifference of random chance. Really, the characters only have two options. Heads or tails. Stay or go. Live or die. Just like us. Just like Hamlet. To be or not to be. Hamlet is not indecisive. He's just upset that the game is rigged. And it's rigged for all of us."

I finish ranting and look up. The room is silent. Total crickets. My classmates regard me with a dazed look. Dr. Dave nods as if he understands me, but I know he doesn't. He can't. He has the look of a man who feels he has always known exactly what the truth is and how to teach it.

"Let's pick this up next time, class," he says.

Everyone moves to gather their books and go.

As I stand up, Aggie is looking at me with a mixture of amusement and concern. She's the only one who gets what I'm saying, of course. The thing about being an identical twin is that you've got an awful lot in common. We enjoy different things, but Agatha is the smartest person I know.

Standing here, facing each other, we're mirror images. Our brown hair is the exact same shade and length, although Aggie likes to wear hers in a perky ponytail. I let mine fall forward and cover half of my face. Her big brown eyes are the same as mine, but she always wears a skim of tasteful liner, whereas I like to pile on the shadow. She's about a quarter of an inch taller than me, but I wear combat boots and she wears ballet flats, so it evens out. Aside from our respective fashion senses (she's preppy, I'm…not), you would never be able to tell us apart.

"Es, do you get the feeling you don't belong?" she asks, smiling at me. "Twin Time™?"

This is a reference to our hours-long gabfests that usually result in us eating way too much ramen and looking up guys on social media. She goes for the

Scandinavian footballer types—big, brawny ones. I prefer the polar opposite.

I don't answer her, even though I feel like I could use some Twin Time™. "Look, I have to split," I say. "I have to meet my advisor about my scholarship."

She narrows her eyes. "How are you doing, by the way? Are you getting better grades?" She's referring to my little problem of doing insanely well in the classes I like and flunking the ones I don't.

"Me? Fine. Just peachy," I answer, avoiding her eyes.

She sighs. "Then I'll see you later? It's your turn to buy food tonight. I want pizza. I'll stop by your room at seven?"

"Fine. See you."

I shoulder my backpack and climb the lecture-theater steps two at a time. I want to get back to the privacy of my dorm room. Back to my poker. Back to the quiet of numbers. I'm supposed to meet my advisor—that part is true. The lie was that I'm not planning to go to the meeting. I have more important things to do.

Chapter Two

Safely back in my single dorm room, I lock the door behind me and head to my Machine. That's what I call my custom-built desktop computer. It has a powerful tower and three ultra-high-definition monitors. I spent nearly a semester's worth of tuition on this sucker. I could probably launch a rocket with this thing, but right now all I need it to do is run my favorite online poker game, Texas Hold'em.

I pull up my playlist and crank the volume. I prefer punky tunes from angry chick bands like Hole and Bikini Kill. The energy keeps me in the right headspace. I need to feel powerful. I'm logged in (my handle is PokerGrrl), and I'm ready to take everyone's money.

"Okay," I say out loud. "Let's see what you've got." I lean back and stretch my arms and shoulders, easing the permanent kink I have in my neck from hunching over my keyboard. Maybe next year I'll get a stand-up desk.

I catch my reflection in the full-length mirror on the back of my dorm-room door. I look tired. I haven't been sleeping much. And my luck hasn't been great. I need to win tonight. I'm down a lot of money.

Even though poker is my drug of choice, it's not just cards that I love. Anything I can bet on will do. And I can find a game anywhere. Horse racing, online games, sports, random bets with strangers—I love it all. I get a rush from the risk and the potential big payoff, but that's not the real draw.

More than anything, I'm attracted to the low of defeat. Because once you get down to the bottom, the only thing left to do is build yourself back up again. That's the part I like best. The comeback. That's the real high.

Trouble is, the stakes are getting so high it's hard to see past them. I know I'm at risk of flunking out, going broke, losing my scholarship and disappointing my parents. I have the two best parents in the universe, by the way. They mortgaged everything so that Aggie and I could study at this great school. An academic scholarship only covers so much. Here I am, on the verge of throwing it all away. I should get up, turn off the Machine and go study in the library. But I can't. Other players are starting to join.

The virtual dealer passes out the two "hole" cards to each player. I get a pair of nines, so I bet pretty hard. I want to raise the pot to weed out the weaker players. Several of them fold, but one remains, a player named BigFish. The dealer then hands out "the flop," the first three of five cards we will share. There's a pair of queens in there. So now I have two pair, queens high. Not bad. It's possible BigFish has a higher pair, but maybe not.

We continue betting and raising. The fourth card, "the turn," is a three, which is probably useless to us both. Then the fifth and final card, "the river," comes out. I am still hoping for another nine, which would give me a full house. It's a jack.

BigFish "checks," which means they pass on betting. I take that as a sign they don't have a great hand. I bet big, hoping they'll fold, but instead BigFish calls my bluff. The pot is now well over $2,000. Our cards are revealed.

I feel like I have been gut-punched.

BigFish had pocket jacks, so a full house, jacks and queens. I'm screwed. I've lost. I am way off my game tonight.

There's a knock at the door. I almost don't hear it over the wailing music. *Crap!* It must be Aggie. Of course it is.

Aggie and her great timing. Good-girl Aggie, future human rights lawyer, all-around angel, and my permanent babysitter. It's really annoying to have an equally smart but overachieving sibling. Especially when they look exactly like you. Sometimes I feel like Aggie got one half of our brain and I got the other, less healthy half. Aggie also got the sweeter personality. I got the darkness.

The knocking continues, louder. After a minute my phone starts to buzz on my desk. I can see it light up with text messages. I peek at it. Yep, Aggie. She hates that I've got her listed as Twinsie. She must be mad because she's shout-texting me:

WHERE R U?
U OWE ME PIZZA BEYOTCH
ES, SERIOUSLY?????

I don't have time for pizza. I have to recoup this loss. I start a new game. I've only got a few hundred dollars left in my account, but if I'm really careful I can build it back up. I can do it. I've just got to focus. I take my lucky coin from my pocket and give it a few flips.

I have some half-hearted thought that I'll play for a little while and then track Aggie down to hang out. But I'm kidding myself. I'll be doing this all night or until whenever I run out of money. I look back at the door, at my reflection, and I almost get up and open it.

Then BigFish makes a huge bet on the new game. The lights and the cards and the flashing dollar signs draw me back in.

When I wake up, I'm still sitting in my computer chair, my head thrown back over the headrest and my neck so kinked that it makes a loud cracking noise as I sit up. The Machine has gone to sleep too, and with shaking hands I reach out and nudge the mouse to see where I left off. I know it can't be good.

I remember losing everything in the middle of the night, even playing online slots in a desperate attempt to win a few dollars back.

When my monitors wake up, my heart falls. It looks like I applied for some credit cards last night too. Great.

I check the time. Seven o'clock. I've got an early-morning chemistry class. I grab my jacket and backpack, a can of coke from my mini fridge and then head out the door.

As I make my way across the quad, I come to a fork in the footpath. One way leads to the science building, and one path leads away to the parking lot (and to the beater car I share with Aggie). I could hop in the car, go get coffee and visit the skate park.

I bet Dillon's there. Dillon from psych class, with the black hair and the long T-shirts always ripped up on the side from his skateboard's grip tape. Dillon with the so-brown-they're-almost-black eyes and the constant dark rings under them that just kill me.

No, I've got to go to class. I've already missed so many. I didn't do the homework—again—and my professor, Dr. Haverly, will call me out for sure. She's always making an example of me, even though the assignments are so basic I can't see the point.

I reach into my jeans pocket and retrieve my lucky coin. I'll flip for it. Heads, I go to class and suffer through the boredom of lessons that are way too easy for me. And keep myself off academic probation for another day. Tails, I go to the skate park and see what kind of mood Dillon is in. He's so hot and cold. Sometimes it seems like he's into me, and other times he acts like I don't exist. I love it.

I flip the coin. *Shit*. It's heads.

"Two out of three," I whisper to myself, flipping the coin again. And then again. Until I get what I want.

Chapter Three

"Cherry or grape?" Dillon is gazing down at me, one corner of his mouth curled up. I'm sitting on the curb on the outer edge of the skate park. I've learned not to hang out near the stairwells and railings because the boarders will come bombing through there to do tricks, whether I'm in the way or not. So I skulk on the sidelines like some kind of pathetic-girlfriend type. Even though Dillon isn't exactly my boyfriend.

I'm not sure what we are. All I know is that he's tall and lean, he's hot as hell, and he switches between giving me laser-focus attention and ignoring me completely. Right now he's got his dark eyes fixed on me. I can't tell where his pupils end and his irises start. He's offering me my choice of lollipop.

Trouble is, I can't decide which flavor I want, and he's looking at me like I'm some kind of curious specimen. I swear he's doing this on purpose. He'll make a terrific shrink one day.

I pull out my coin and flip for it. "Heads I choose cherry," I say. When it lands heads up, his smile deepens.

"Here you go. Cherry," he says, his voice low, his cool gaze never breaking contact.

I swallow. "Thanks," I say, unwrapping the candy. I'm acutely aware of him watching me as I put the lollipop in my mouth. If I were Aggie, I'd look straight at him while I do this. She's bold that way with guys. I'm not. Being me, being Ester, I shove it into my mouth as fast as possible and look at my feet. I'm all bravery during a poker game, but when it comes to Dillon I'm hopeless.

"So what's with the coin, sugar?" Dillon asks as he sits down on his skateboard next to me. He kind of rolls toward me a bit and reaches his arm around my side to keep from smashing into my hip. I flinch a little but am pleased when he doesn't let go. I'm still reeling a little bit from him calling me "sugar."

"Um," I say, finding my courage. "Sugar?"

"No, Chigurgh," he says and spells it out.

"Huh?"

"The Coen brothers movie?"

"What?"

"You know, that movie about the total psycho who goes around flipping coins, making people choose heads or tails and then killing them with, like, an air-gun thing? You have better hair though," he adds, sucking on his own lollipop with lips that are criminally full.

"I don't...watch many movies," I say.

"Yeah, I can tell." That crooked smile again.

I must look offended, because he's quick to apologize. "Hey," he says. "I didn't mean it like that. I just mean you're so smart and young. You're, like, this really studious kid, you know."

Kid. Great. "So, what, you're ultra-mature?" I ask, my voice betraying just how irritated I am by the whole "kid" comment.

"I am three years older than you," he says.

"Yeah, and you get everywhere on a skateboard."

"It's better for the environment than your jalopy over there," he says, jerking his head toward the old Volkswagen Rabbit Aggie and I share. The hair on his forehead flops forward, and I nearly die.

"Jalopy?" I tease. "What are you, a hundred years old?"

He laughs. "Good one, babe."

Babe. He's never called me that.

He gets up and takes a sudden run on the rails,

nailing it. As he skates past, I see two guys in tracksuits walk by the stairs, heading toward the pedestrian overpass.

When I flipped my coin deciding to come here, I was kidding myself that it was to see Dillon. Really, it's to see them. As hot as Dillon is, and as much as I hate my boring classes, the allure of an illegal poker game is stronger.

I grab my backpack and walk over. Out of the corner of my eye I can see Dillon is focused on landing a trick. I don't want him to see me talking to these guys, so I hurry after them under the overpass.

One of the tracksuit guys, John Jr., nods at me, his shaved head glistening with sweat. He always looks like he's been up late partying, hungover as hell. Maybe he is. Owning an after-hours club probably has its drawbacks.

His brother, Big Steve, who's actually quite short, shorter than me, turns and gives me a sly smile. His shoulders are about as wide as he is tall, and he's clearly skipping leg day. He has the physique of a walking triangle, and I can't help but try to calculate his angles in my mind. According to my math, he shouldn't even be able to stand up. How does he not tip over? He's a marvel of modern trigonometry.

"What's up, Essssssssie?" he hisses, drawing out my name in a way that I think *he* thinks is cute. He's always looking me up and down. John Jr. told me once that I could get a bigger stake in the game if I let Big Steve take me out. I politely declined, saying I was busy with school. My guy preferences run much more along the tall rectangular spectrum.

I peek around the corner to glance over at the skate bowl. Dillon is sitting on his board at the ledge, chewing gum and talking to a couple friends. I watch his jaw clench and imagine what it would be like to just walk over there and kiss him the way I want to.

"Who's that guy you're eyeballing?" John Jr. asks in his typically flat monotone.

"He's in my class," I say. "I'm going to ask him for his notes." Lying is coming easier and easier these days. It just rolls off my tongue.

John Jr. seems to accept this with a dismissive wave of his hand. "Meh," he says. "What good is school for a girl like you, huh? You should just come work for us. With your...skills."

Big Steve laughs, leering at me. "Yeah, good one. Her *skills*."

John Jr. rolls his eyes. "Math skills, Stevo, math. This girl's outta your league."

"Speaking of which," I say. "You guys have a game going tonight?"

John Jr. nods, his gaze landing on another beat-up car that has pulled up to the curb. It's a kind of sunset-tan color, somehow even uglier than my green VW.

I'm guessing it's someone looking for the bad party drugs Big Steve likes to deal on the side.

"Can I get in on that game?" I ask. *Please say yes, please say yes, please say yes.*

John Jr. sighs. "Kid, you can't afford this one."

My pulse quickens. A challenge. Just how big *is* this game? I play it cool. "How do you know what I can afford?"

John Jr. cocks an eyebrow at me and chuckles. "All right. A thousand to buy in. After that, it's sudden death. No credit. You run out of cash and you're out, understand?"

I nod. Wow, that's a lot.

"So what's it going to be?" he asks.

I should run away, back to campus, to Aggie, tell her everything, ask for her help. I should definitely, positively, not try to get a stake in this game. No, nope, uh-uh.

I sigh and reach for my lucky coin.

Chapter Four

This Italian restaurant I'm sitting in, Rosso's, just off campus, is the closest thing to home cooking Aggie and I have. With our parents and extended family a three-hour drive away, we might as well be stranded on the moon. Italian families like ours bond over big meals, and the food can't be just okay. It has to be incredible. I yearn for my mom's ziti, and Aggie hungers for our dad's secret-recipe spaghetti with basil. The next best thing is Rosso's and the kindly older Italian couple who run the place.

I'm waiting for Aggie to get off work at the nearby coffee shop. I watch for her through the rain-speckled window facing the street. Every time I look up, I see my reflection staring back at me.

Fall here isn't some red-leaved, pumpkin-patched, cozy hot-chocolate commercial. It's a dreary, gray, rainy slog of a place. I watch people walk by. Every one of them seems to move with a purpose, like they've got somewhere or someone important to get to. Every person I see has a nicely coordinated outfit with appropriate outerwear. When they get wherever they're going, they'll be snug and dry and safe and perfect. The opposite of me, I think.

I shrug off the damp hoodie I've been using as a jacket and feel the cold squish of my wet socks through my Vans. One more thing I couldn't budget for—rain gear. Man, when your life is falling apart, it's so obvious how much other people are winning at things compared to you.

Just as I'm thinking about taking off, I see another face beside my own in the window. But this face is smiling. And dry. Because this face belongs to Aggie, and she's wearing Gore-Tex.

I fiddle with my lucky coin as she hustles in, bringing the smell of rain and wet asphalt and clean hair with her.

"Hey," she says, flopping down. "You order already?"

"Uh, no," I say. "I didn't know what you wanted."

Aggie frowns at this obvious lie. Of course I know what she wants. She always gets the same thing— spaghetti and a starter of marinated squid. I always get the lasagna, and I usually steal a few pieces of Aggie's appetizer.

What she doesn't know is that I didn't order because I'm broke. If she hadn't shown up, I wouldn't have been able to pay. And I'm not going to leave Mr. and Mrs. Rosso high and dry. They've been too kind to us.

"What's wrong?" Aggie asks, her eyes skimming over me as if she can divine the truth.

I shrug. I open my mouth to speak, but nothing comes out.

"Ester," she says. "What is it?"

Just then Mr. Rosso shuffles over with a basket of bread and a plate of balsamic vinegar and oil.

"How are the Tomasi twins tonight?" he says, chuckling. He says this every time we come in.

"Hi, Mr. Rosso," Aggie says, flashing him her best grown-up-pleasing smile.

I smile too, but it's more like forcing the corners of my mouth upward into a kind of grimace.

"The usual?" he asks.

"You bet!" says Aggie.

"Uh-huh," I manage.

"Good," says Mr. Rosso. "Because Mrs. Rosso already started your order." He turns and walks away.

Aggie giggles. "So cute," she says.

"Listen, Ag, I don't have any cash on me. Can you cover my lasagna?"

"Sure," she says. "I actually got some tips today."

"Thanks," I mutter.

We eat the bread in silence until the rest of our food comes. When I bite into the lasagna, it's so good I feel like crying.

Aggie starts telling me about some coffee-shop drama, but my mind flashes back to John Jr. and Big Steve. And the money I need to buy in. A thousand bucks. A game like this could put me back in the black for a long time.

I flip my coin and turn it over in my hand.

Aggie looks up from her spaghetti with a worried look. "What are we deciding today, Es?"

It's so like her to know what I'm thinking. Twin Telepathy™.

"I, um, overspent some of my money."

Aggie is shaking her head at me. "What? Don't tell me you bought more ridiculous computer equipment."

"You got me," I say. It feels disgusting to look my twin in the face and lie to her.

Aggie sighs. "Are you going to be able to make tuition?"

"It could be tight," I say. "And nothing left over for books or food or anything."

"Ester," she scolds.

"I know. I've learned my lesson. I just need some help, Ag."

She shrugs. "Well, how much?"

"Like, a thousand," I say quietly.

"A thousand dollars?" Aggie screeches.

"I'm sorry."

"That's a lot. If I give it to you, then I'm going to be eating nothing but ramen next semester."

"Yeah, I understand."

She smiles. "But I *like* ramen, so..."

"So you'll do it?"

"On one condition," she says.

"What?" I ask.

"The car. I'm the one who takes care of it, remembers to insure it, gets the oil changed, pays for most of the gas..." She trails off.

"You want the VW?"

"I'll still give you rides, of course," she says. "But it's hard for me to get to my job and get back in time to study. It would be easier for me this way. And you don't really need it, right? You hang out on campus or stalk that skateboarder guy."

"Dillon," I say, and we both start laughing.

"He's not my type," she says. "But he is *fiiiiine*."

"Oh my god, I know."

"So it's a deal then?" she asks.

"Deal." I am feeling that jittery thrill again.

We dig in to the rest of our meals. Aggie returns to jabbering about work. She just loves to talk. And talk. She's going to make a great lawyer one day.

I'm barely listening. I won't be able to concentrate on anything until I have that thousand dollars in my account. No matter what, I won't be leaving Rosso's before Aggie e-transfers the funds to me. That goes without saying. You can bet on it.

Chapter Five

The e-transfer doesn't have a hold on it. Luckily, I applied for an overdraft at my bank a few months ago, when my bank account was in better shape. I try to ignore how my hands shake as I pull the cash from the ATM.

I head to the game. It's almost 2:00 a.m., which is when the club closes officially. I want to get there as soon as possible. For one thing, it's making me nervous to be walking around with so much cash in my pocket.

Every time I walk past someone, I think I'm about to be mugged, even though this area of town is made up of mostly hipster college students. Their monthly coffee budgets are greater than my dorm fees. I wonder what would happen if I did get robbed. You're supposed to give up the money, let the mugger have it, but there's no way I could do that. I'd die first.

I get to the bus stop and wait, anxiously hoping the night bus comes soon. I see that weird golden-tan car that was at the skate park. It's idling just down the road, its headlights off. A dark figure sits inside. And I could have sworn I saw this same car drive by when I was waiting for Aggie at Rosso's. I'm totally paranoid. *Less coffee, more sleep, Ester. Get out of my brain, Aggie.*

Just then a hand grabs my shoulder and I yelp, spinning around.

"Whoa!" Dillon exclaims, putting his hands up. He's trying not to laugh. "I didn't mean to scare you, kid."

"What the hell, Dillon! You don't sneak up on girls. Not at night. Not at the freaking bus stop. Not when—" I stop before I reveal too much. I keep *that* to myself.

He gives me a soft smile. "I am really sorry. I wasn't thinking. You forgive me?" When he says this last part, he dips his head lower, his hair flops forward (oh my god, that dark hair), and he kind of bites his lip. I'm done for. He knows exactly what he's doing.

I can't stop the smile from spreading across my face. "You're forgiven," I say. "But on probation," I add, and he laughs. "What are you doing out here so late?"

"I was out with some guys from my psych lab. Real fun time," he says. "What are you doing here?" he asks. "Jalopy break down?"

I shake my head. "Nope. Aggie needs it more right now. So I gave it up."

"Oh, well, that's nice of you," he says.

If he only knew.

"Bonus for me," he continues. "I run into you just when I was thinking about you."

"You were thinking about me?" My heart starts thumping harder.

"Yeah, I was hoping we could hang. You want to go grab a very, very late night? Or just, you know, chill at my place?" He stares into my eyes, and his gaze feels like it has all the gravity of the earth behind it. He has pinned me to this point in space.

Food with Dillon, hanging with Dillon—anything with Dillon—sounds amazing. But the weight of the money in my pocket, and the call of the poker game, is too much to resist.

"I'd love to," I say, already mentally kicking myself for turning him down, "but I just have somewhere to be."

"At this ungodly hour?" he asks. "Another fella? Who is this mystery beau?"

I laugh. "How could I be interested in another guy when I have this handsome old-timer here with me?"

"You jest," he says. "But I'm timeless. And..."

He trails off. "Es, I want to go on a real date with you. I like it when we hang out. A date would be cool."

"So you want to bring me a corsage and meet my dad?" I tease, like what he just said is no big deal. Oh my god.

"Yep, afraid so. I'm traditional that way, being 104 years old or whatever."

"Um…" I'm speechless for a second. I can hear Aggie's voice in my mind: *Answer him, Es.* Dillon is staring down at me, standing so close, chewing on that bottom lip.

"Yes!" I practically shout, then quickly try to regain whatever sense of cool I had.

Dillon grins. "Cool. You like hockey?"

Not really, no. "Um, yeah? Doesn't everyone?"

"I have tickets for tomorrow's game. We can grab a bite to eat after, if you want," he suggests.

"Okay," I say. "Or we can…chill." My heart pounds. I can't believe I just said that. Essie would be proud.

He laughs. "Great."

"Great."

I hear the bus rumbling down the street, and I turn to step toward the curb, but Dillon reaches out and grabs my hand. He pulls me closer to him. As the bus glides in beside us, he leans down and gives me a kiss. Not on the lips, not on the cheek, but right on my neck, just below my left ear. My legs almost go out from under me.

"Your bus is here," he whispers as the doors hiss open.

"Yeah," I manage. "Okay. Um, bye."

"Bye," he says, keeping his eyes locked on me as I fumble for change and try to step up onto the bus without looking as flustered as I feel inside.

I grab a seat near the front of the bus and look out the window, past my own reflection, to see that Dillon is watching me. He's waiting for the bus to leave. How could I have known this rascal of a guy would also be kind of a gentleman?

The bus pulls away and accelerates down the street. I resist the urge to look back to see if Dillon is still there. I almost manage it but have to sneak a quick glance.

He has started gliding down the sidewalk on his skateboard.

I watch him pass a car. That same tan car. Its headlights come on, and it drives away.

I try to push my paranoid thoughts from my mind.

I have a poker game to win.

Chapter Six

I am going to lose this game.

I had to hand over my thousand dollars to John Jr. when I walked in the back door of the club. Before I'd even had a chance to see who was going to be playing.

Now that I'm inside and sitting in the middle of the action, I can see that I'm way out of my league. John Jr. did try to warn me, but like he's going to turn down easy money.

The room is smoky, filled with the blue haze from cigars. It chokes me and makes my eyes burn. I very stupidly forgot to wear sunglasses, so now my eyes are exposed to everyone at the table. They're all men, all older than me and all wearing dark shades.

I can smell the testosterone in the room. I know what each of them is thinking as they sit and look at me across the smooth green felt of the players' table. I'm a new fish, someone to knock out of the action early and without pity. I'd think the same thing.

I take a deep breath. No, I'm not going to psych myself out of this. I have to remember that these guys may be older, or more experienced, but I've probably got the highest IQ in the room. I just have to be careful. Keep it conservative. *Don't get carried away. Don't get sucked into going all in too quickly.*

I've only got my thousand-dollar stake, plus a few hundred I was able to scrounge from my overdraft and the remains of some credit-card cash advances. It's going to have to last me a while. I have a pretty

43

small stack of chips in front of me. The guys all have huge stacks.

"Sheila!" John Jr. bellows to a server wearing a skimpy skirt and bikini top. "Bring drinks for our players."

The server saunters over to me first. "What'll you have, sweetie?" she asks kindly.

"Uh, ginger ale, please," I say. The men all laugh.

Let them. Let them order their double scotches and their shots of cold Russian vodka. It will only help me.

"Stevo," says John Jr. "Let's get this action started."

"Okay," says Stevo, opening the door. A small bald man in a crisp white shirt enters. He's carrying a metal case.

The man sits down in the dealer position, opens his case, and removes several sealed packages of cards. He opens them and begins shuffling. Moments later he inserts them into his card-dealing machine.

He looks around the table at all of us. His gaze falls briefly on me. Abruptly he gets up and approaches John Jr. They speak in hushed tones. After a minute the dealer throws his hands up and returns to the table, shaking his head. He glances at me, and if I'm not mistaken, I see a slight look of concern on his face.

He quickly explains the rules, but we all know them. Every single one of us is anxious for the game to start. Despite all our differences, we have this in common. We love poker. We can't live without it. Gambling is like breathing. We need this.

"Post your blinds," the dealer instructs. We all push forward the required chips.

He deals out the hole cards, and I wait a moment before looking at mine. Instead, I watch the faces of the men as they check their cards. Some are animated, making a show of being happy or pissed off at the results, but there's no way to know if their emotions are genuine. I spot a couple of bad actors right away and figure they are bluffing. But at this level, it could be a double bluff.

A couple of players are steely-faced and reveal nothing, barely glancing at their cards long enough to see what they have. This can also be a "tell"—a way for me to figure out whether they have a good hand or not. One of these guys, silver-haired with deep forehead creases and a pair of gold sunglasses, keeps so still he seems like a statue. But the fingers on his right hand twitch. I decide it is a sign he has a monster hand. Probably pocket aces. He's itching to bet.

I inhale, calming myself, and carefully lift the corners of my cards. I've got a ten and a queen, both clubs. It's not terrible, and it could be great, but it all depends on the flop.

We go around the table, placing bets. Two players fold right away. When it comes to me I "check" because my hand isn't strong enough to bet on. I want to see what Golden Sunglasses will do. I expect him to bet, but he checks too.

Now I'm sure he has a good hand. He's trying to lure me in. I may have to fold after the flop.

The dealer lays out the three cards. A two of hearts, a seven of diamonds and an ace of clubs. I glance at Golden Sunglasses, and he's as still as before.

Betting starts again, and the other players fold out of the game, leaving it to me and Golden Sunglasses. It's his turn, so he makes a modest bet, a hundred dollars. Big enough to be serious but small enough that he could still be bluffing.

Now what do I do? Worst-case scenario is he's got two aces in the hole and one showing in the flop. He could have three of a kind. And I've got nothing, really. But I have the makings of a straight flush. I just need the king and the jack of clubs. I know the odds aren't good. About 1 in 30,940, actually.

You know what? I'm here to play. I need to establish myself at this table. And so I see his bet and raise it another $50. He sees my raise, and the dealer adds another card. When I see the turn, my heart nearly stops. It's a jack of clubs. I stay very still, trying not to reveal any feelings whatsoever. I glance at Golden Sunglasses. I know he's staring at me, even though I can't see his eyes.

The action is on me. I'm not sure where this is going, so I check again.

Golden Sunglasses takes this as a sign I've got nothing (technically he's right), and he places a big bet. Five hundred dollars. He's trying to take me out on my first hand. He marked me from the get-go.

I could fold and be out a couple hundred but stay alive for a few more hands. Or I could see his bet. Hell, I could go all in on my very first hand and hope the river card is the one I need to win this.

My skin starts to prickle. I can feel sweat running down the middle of my back. It's hot in here. Cigar smoke is seeping into my pores. Do I bet it all? The probability that this final card is the one I need is 1 in 43,316.

I look at Golden Sunglasses and notice the slightest smirk flash across his mouth. It's a blink-or-you-miss-it expression, but I see it. I decide to go for it.

I push my chips forward. All of them. "All in," I say. My voice is a squeak.

Golden Sunglasses shakes his head at me a little and then matches my raise. He's calling me out.

The dealer speaks. "Cards up," he instructs. We both have to reveal our hands.

Golden Sunglasses turns his over, and my heart sinks. He does, in fact, have two aces.

"Three of a kind, aces," declares the dealer.

Everyone is paying attention now. I turn mine over. There is an audible intake of breath and a few murmurs.

I'm one card away from a straight flush, a royal flush, the hand to beat all hands.

Golden Sunglasses is staring hard at me right now. "You got balls, little fish," he grumbles. "Let's see if you're lucky."

"I've got something better than balls," I say, finding my courage.

All the men stare at me. "Ovaries," I say, as if it isn't obvious.

Big Steve laughs his obnoxious guffaw, and that's when I realize that he and John Jr. have been watching the action with fascination.

"Here comes the river," says the dealer. He pulls the card from the machine.

His hand seems to move in slow motion as he turns it over and places it on the table.

It's black. Oh my god. It's a king. It's a club.

I've just won almost $2,000.

"Jesus Christ," mutters Golden Sunglasses.

"Winner, straight flush," declares the dealer, handing me stacks of chips.

"Thank you," I say. It's going to be a fun night.

Chapter Seven

This is not fun anymore.

I had a few good hands, and I'm up almost ten grand. It's not enough to cover every debt I have, but it's a damn good start. I could walk away and scrape by for the rest of the year without anyone, least of all Aggie, knowing just how bad it was.

It's just…there's another big pot brewing. Golden Sunglasses and a skinny guy who looks like

Steve Buscemi have bet huge. If I can win it, I'll be totally free and clear.

The problem isn't my hand. I've got a pair of fours, and the flop is showing a pair of tens and a four. The turn card is a five. So I've got a full house, fours and tens. The problem is, I don't know what my opponents have.

They could just have pairs or three of a kind. Either way, my full house would beat them. The nightmare would be if one of them has a better full house than mine, with higher cards. The odds of that are less than 3 percent, and the odds of them having four of a kind are less than 1 percent.

Do I bet on those odds? I almost fold, but something stops me. I can't walk away from this. I can't leave with an okay win when big money is still in play. I've got to go double or nothing.

Before I can change my mind, I push all my chips forward. "All in," I say, proud that my voice didn't waver.

I see the dealer frown.

Steve Buscemi folds. It's too rich for his blood. It's down to Golden Sunglasses again. This time he's smiling.

He pushes his stack of chips forward, calling me. Then he flips his cards over. All the air seems to leave the room. There's no sound, save for the pounding of my heart. It's just me and my intense regret.

Golden Sunglasses has pocket tens. So four of a kind. He wins. With shaking hands I turn over my cards. His smile grows.

"I knew I'd get you eventually, little fish," he says.

I'm going to puke.

I turn to talk to John Jr., to beg him for an additional stake, but he must have stepped out. It's just Big Steve, leering at me.

"Hey, Big Steve. Can you help a girl out?"

He shakes his head. "You know what Junior said. Once you're out, you're out. No credit."

I can feel the bile rise in my throat. "But it's me. Come on. You don't always have to do what he says, right?"

Big Steve stares at me for a long moment and then looks over his shoulder. "Fine, girlie," he says. "Another grand."

I sigh with relief. "Thank you so much."

He calls over to the dealer. "A thousand to the little lady."

The dealer sighs and counts out the chips.

Another round starts, and then another, and I do okay—until I am losing again. It's nothing dramatic. No big hands, just a gradual slide. I ask for more and more chips, until I'm in the hole at least three grand.

On my last hand I only have enough to post blinds before I'm all in again. I've got nothing. Steve Buscemi beats me with a pair of sevens.

"Hey, better luck next time," he offers, avoiding my gaze. I'm just trying not to cry.

John Jr. walks back into the room, carrying a pizza.

"Aw, what happened, Essie?" he asks with mock concern. "You get knocked out by the big boys?"

I grab my bag and leave the table, heading for the door, but Big Steve steps in my way. *Shit.*

"Whoa there, girlie. What about our three large?" he asks.

"What the hell?" John Jr. snarls. "Stevo, tell me you didn't loan this girl any dough."

He shrugs. "The little girl made her bed. Now she can lie in it."

I've always said that I love the low of defeat. That there's nothing like getting down so far into the abyss that you think you'll never get out. That it's kind of great because you get to claw your way back up to the light? I take that back. This is not love. It's misery.

John Jr. fixes his steely gaze on me. "You going to come up with my money, kid?"

"I'm good for it. I can get it," I lie.

"Good. You have until the end of the week. After that we come to you. You understand what that means?"

I swallow hard and nod.

The walk home is long and cold. I don't even have any change for the bus, and the night is already fading away to dawn. I pull my hoodie tighter around myself, trying to fight off the deep chill that has settled into my bones. It's all too real to be a nightmare.

Once I'm back in my dorm, I look around for things I can sell. My Machine. It's used, but if I can get a local student to buy parts, I could make cash fast. I open my jewelry box and take out anything gold, including some small rings that my dad gave me when I was little. It won't be enough.

I plop down on my bed. I'm going to have to ask my parents for a loan. I look at the clock. Six a.m. Dad should be up for work. I call his cell, half hoping he won't answer. He does. He always does.

"Hi there, favorite twin!" Dad always calls me this. I'm sure he calls Aggie this too, but he'll never admit it.

"Hi, Dad," I say, sounding as tired as I feel.

"It's so early! Catching the worm, sweetheart?"

"Something like that. Um, Dad, I have a problem."

"Oh? Everything okay, Ester?" His concern radiates through the phone.

"Yeah, everything's fine. It's just...there's been a delay in my student funding," I say. "So I'm broke until it comes through, and I've got to pay for next semester soon."

"Oh jeez, honey. How are you surviving?" he asks.

I bite my lip to keep from crying. "I'm okay. I just need an advance, and then I can pay you back when the funding comes in. A couple weeks, tops."

"Well, I'm sure I could move some things around. I'll go to the bank on my way to work and transfer you some money. How much do you need?"

"Well, with tuition and everything...like, $4,000," I say. It's not nearly enough, but it would pay off John Jr. and Big Steve and leave me something to live on.

"Whoa, honey," he says. "That's a lot to come up with so fast."

"I know," I say. "I'm so sorry."

"I can get you a thousand today and a little more later. Could you talk to financial services and ask them to make an exception? I mean, the delay isn't your fault. I could call them myself—" he says.

"No!" I interject. "That's totally fine. A thousand is great. No problem," I say.

"Okay, sweetheart. Well, I've got to get to work, honey. I'll talk to you later. Give my love to Agatha, yes?"

"Okay, Dad. I will. Love you too." I barely get the words out before hanging up.

I fall back onto my bed. The room is reeling. I'm exhausted, but it takes forever to fall asleep. When I finally do, I don't dream.

Chapter Eight

I sleep until noon and wake with a jolt. I check my online account and see that Dad has come through.

I take a few photos of my Machine and post them in an online marketplace for our campus. It isn't long before someone DMs me, asking for a price. We haggle a bit, and I sell the entire setup for $900. It's a fraction of what it's worth, but I have no choice. I carefully wipe the hard drive and reset it to factory mode.

The kid who bought it shows up fifteen minutes later with a rolling dolly. As I help him load up my Machine, I can't help feeling like a sucker. He pays cash like it's nothing to him. Envy stabs through me like a knife.

I'm almost two-thirds of the way to paying off the gangsters. Maybe they'll take a payment plan, I think as I head to the local pawnshop. I've put everything of any value that I own in my backpack.

The U-Pawn shelves are lined with MP3 players, computer parts and similar things a desperate college student would hock.

The man behind the counter looks like an old ship's captain. I dislike him right away. He peruses my items, turning over the jewelry and inspecting it with a pinched look on his face.

"I'll give you two hundred for everything," he says at last.

I gasp. "$200? That's *it*?"

He shrugs. "Take it or leave it."

"But..." I hold up a small gold ring with an emerald in it. "This ring was a gift from my dad. It's special."

He shakes his head. "Then maybe you should keep it."

He takes out a scale and places the ring on it. "It's by weight," he says. "Not by feelings. And this tiny piece of gold is worth about fifteen bucks."

Fifteen bucks? I need this money so bad. What am I going to do? I take out my lucky coin and flip it a few times.

He leans forward and watches as it lands face up on my palm. "Hey, now that's interesting," Captain Pawn says. "Let me see that."

"No!" I put the coin in my pocket. "My grandpa gave it to me before he died."

"Suit yourself," he says. "You want the two hundred or not?"

I nod, watching as he takes my possessions away and lays out the cash on the smudged glass counter.

I grab the money and my pawn ticket and get the hell out of there. When I have enough money, I'll buy it all back. Every last thing.

Selling my most prized possessions took longer than I thought, and I don't have enough time to try to find John Jr. and Big Steve before my date with Dillon. I'll just have to take the money to them later at the club.

I text Dillon that I'm running late.

He suggests we meet outside the gate at the arena.

See you soon

Later, kid

Will you stop calling me kid?

Ok babe.

Oh my god.

I hurry to the bus stop and arrive just as my bus pulls in. I actually have some cash now, so I'm able to pay the fare. I might even buy Dillon a pretzel at the game. He did mention liking them.

I slide into my seat, clutching my bag close to me. Stuffed inside is every cent I have. I pull out my compact and give myself a once-over. Hair, a little greasy but decent. Face, shiny as hell. A quick swipe of HD powder. Lips, forever chapped. I pull out my Dr. Pepper Lip Smackers lip balm and smear it on. So tasty, and the perfect sheer brownish-red color. I pick out an eye crust and check my teeth. Look okay. It's not like I've eaten anything of substance for...how long has it been? Maybe I'll grab a pretzel too. I pop a piece of mint gum in my mouth and try to relax for the rest of the bus ride.

By the time I get to the arena, the place is packed. I worry I won't be able to find Dillon in the crowd. But he stands out in the best way. As the sea of people filters through the gates, I spot him. Tall, dark, dressed in black, leaning with a casual indifference against one of the barriers.

I have the impulse to turn and run away. I'm so into him, but I wonder if I'm the kind of girl he needs. He's got his life together. He's on track. I'm a mess.

Dillon sees me before I can leave. "Essie!" he calls out, his face breaking into that crooked grin that dissolves any thoughts I had of leaving.

He strides over. "Hey," he says, reaching in to give me a hug.

When his arms wrap around me, I fall into him, until he's supporting the full weight of me with his own long body. He's so warm.

"Hey," he says again, softer this time. "You really know how to hug."

"Warm," I murmur.

He laughs.

We pull away, and I feel shy until he takes my hand.

"Ready for some hockey?" he asks.

"Sure." I let him lead me inside.

The game is...well, the game. I honestly don't know what's going on, other than the fact that our team is winning. Dillon is stoked, and I can't take my eyes off him as he eats his pretzel. He chews with those lips I love and hoots with excitement whenever one of the players does something good.

No matter how adorable Dillon is, my mind can't stop drifting to the cash in my bag. I should get it to the gangsters, pay down as much as possible, beg for more time, get myself straight and just be a boring college student from now on.

I've noticed some guys moving through the crowd with their notebooks, hanging around the bathrooms. Shifty eyes and hard faces. Drug dealers, some of them. And some of them are bookies.

Just watch the game, Ester. Focus on Dillon. Aggie's in my head again.

As if on cue, my phone buzzes. Of course it's Aggie. Ugh. ALL CAPS again.

HEY I TALKED TO DAD.

WHY DID YOU NEED MONEY FROM HIM TOO?

ARE YOU GOING TO PAY ME BACK?

WHAT IS GOING ON WITH YOU?

ESTER I SWEAR...

I can't deal with this right now. If Aggie finds out the truth, I'll never live down the shame. She'll make me feel guilty for the rest of my life. I feel anger boiling in my stomach.

"Hey," I shout to Dillon over the noise. "I'll be right back. Bathroom."

"Want me to come?" he shouts back.

I shake my head, wave him off and head up the aisle.

It takes me two minutes to find the guy. I've never met this bookie, but we know each other all the same. He's real greasy-looking, and he nods for me to follow him into the accessible washroom.

"It's late in the game," he says.

"I know." Am I really doing this?

"I'll only stake a long shot."

"Meaning?"

"You gotta bet against home winning, and it's gotta be by a minimum of two points, or no deal."

"But home is winning."

"Exactly."

I sigh. "What's the payout?"

"Three to one," he says.

I fish out my cash and hand him everything I've got. If I win, I can pay off the gangsters and be up a bit.

"You sure, kid?" he asks, but he's already pocketing the money. He hands me a slip of paper. "If you win, this is how you collect."

"Thanks," I mutter and hurry back to my seat. I'm suddenly very interested in the game.

As I watch the players fighting to win, and the crowd cheering them on, I think about how I will always find myself here. It's not about the money. It's not even about winning or losing. It's about hating myself, punishing myself and then seeking redemption in all the wrong ways. I usually have these moments of clarity after I've made a decision I can't come back from. Once I've made it through, I'll forget all over again.

Now, instead of enjoying a date with Dillon, I'm focused on the impossible. I've bet it all against the home team. Before I can even wrap my mind around it, the buzzer sounds and the game is over. The home team wins. And I lose.

As the crowd goes wild around me, cheering and screaming and waving colored towels, their jerseys a sea of ecstatic blue and white and green, I feel like I've left my body. I have the sensation of floating above the crowd and seeing Dillon grab me. I watch as he presses his lips into mine, and I think, How sad that I can't be here to feel this.

But I am here. This is my life. For how much longer, I don't know.

Chapter Nine

The next several days are a waking nightmare. I'm so exhausted from not sleeping that I keep falling asleep everywhere and then jolting awake as if I've been shocked. Strange, static bolts zip up the back of my neck, and my fingers and feet tingle. It hurts, and I wonder if a person can die from stress. The few classes I've tried to attend have ended in disaster. I can't concentrate, can't speak when called upon and spend the whole time trying not to throw up before bolting out of the room.

Aggie has been stalking me, waiting outside my classes to try to intercept me. I dodge her yet again but decide to finally text her back.

> *Sorry. Super busy.*
>
> You can't avoid me 4ever. You owe me big-time!
>
> *Thanks for not ratting me out to Mom and Dad.*
>
> Need 2 meet up and talk. No Twin Time in weeks!
>
> *I'll meet u tonight. I'm bringing Dillon. U guys can finally meet. But u have to be good!*
>
> Whatever. Fine. Bring yr man.
>
> *Agatha. Promise. Don't embarrass me.*
>
> Ok I promise. If u stand me up again, all bets are off.

I think I've managed to get her off my back. The only thing I have to worry about now is that everywhere I go, I see John Jr. and Big Steve. Am I cracking up? I see them in reflections on windows. I catch a glimpse of a tracksuited guy in a hallway. Sometimes I think I see that suspicious tan car again too. I wonder if it's someone who works for them. Are they following me?

I've been staying at Dillon's a lot, getting lost in him. In his dark eyes and his long body and the things he knows how to do. I could kiss him for a thousand years.

I like everything about Dillon's off-campus apartment. He shares it with a couple other guys, and it's messy, but I'm pleased to see that he has a ton of books. We stay up late watching old movies and making out and more. So much more. I can see how easily Dillon could become an addiction all on his own. He even has a taste I crave.

It's at the coffee shop, when I'm waiting for Aggie to get off work and for Dillon to show up, that John Jr. and Big Steve finally come for me.

I look up from my latte and watch as John Jr. approaches my table in the back corner. Big Steve loiters near the doorway, cracking his knuckles.

They stick out in their flashy clothes, amid all the hipsters with beards. For a second I wonder if I should run. I cast a nervous glance over to the coffee bar to see if Aggie is watching, but she's absorbed in her job.

John Jr. puts out his hand and motions for me to stay put. "Relax, kid," he says. "We're just here to talk."

I look past him to Big Steve. Just beyond him, on the street, is that weird tan car. It *does* belong to them!

"H-hi, John Jr.," I manage. "Listen, I'm really sorry—"

"Save it," he snaps. "You think this has never happened before?" He leans in so close that I can smell his cologne.

I swallow hard.

"Look. I like you, kid. And my idiot brother never should've staked you in that game. But you made your choice. You could've walked away with a fine pot. Instead you blew it."

"I'm sorry," I whisper. "I have a problem."

John Jr. nods. "You're right you gotta problem. And it's gonna get a lot worse if I don't get my money."

Big Steve waddles over, turning sideways to get through the crowded shop, a smarmy smile on his face. "I can think of a way for her to pay off her debt," he says. "With that pretty face and young body."

My whole body goes cold. *No, anything but that.*

John Jr. looks irritated. "Shut up, Stevo." Then he says to me, "But he is right. Either you come up with the money in one week, all of it, or you gotta come work for us."

Work for him? "I...how?"

"You're a pretty girl. You can come work after hours, help the patrons get liquored up. Encourage them to gamble more," he says.

My mind flashes to the cocktail waitress who served me ginger ale at the poker game. "You mean in a bikini?" I squeak.

Big Steve laughs.

"Of course, we have other things on offer besides poker games and booze," says John Jr. "Things your rich college friends might want."

I get it now. They want me to sell drugs.

"One week. You'll get all of it. I promise."

"One week," John Jr. repeats as they turn to go. He nods his head toward the coffee bar. "Or we pay a visit to her first. To Agatha."

My blood turns to ice at the mention of her name. Not Aggie. I shake my head furiously, but John Jr. just smiles a cold smile as he leaves. They walk out the door just as Dillon arrives.

He heads over to me, a strange look on his face. I'm dreading his questions.

"Hey." He leans in to give me a quick kiss on the forehead.

I can barely feel it. My whole body has gone numb.

"What were those guys doing here?" he asks.

I shrug. "What guys?"

Dillon sits down and stares at me. "Es, I saw them talking to you."

"Oh...that one guy, the short and muscly one, is always asking me out."

Dillon considers this. "Okay," he says at last. "I was worried maybe you were on drugs." He narrows his eyes. "Because that's not cool with me."

I laugh it off. "Of course not," I say. "I'm on an academic scholarship. I'm not on drugs."

"Right," he says. "You're a smarty-pants. That's why I like you," he adds, sliding closer to me. He starts to kiss me, but we're interrupted by Aggie.

"Ahem," she says in a dramatic way.

"Great timing, as usual," I say as we pull apart.

"You must be Aggie," says Dillon, standing up to offer his hand. Ever the gentleman.

"I am." Aggie smiles. "And you must be the infamous Dillon."

Chapter Ten

Coffee is...fine. It is a little painful having Aggie and Dillon both together in the same room. Aggie learns all about Dillon's passion for skateboarding, and Dillon learns all about...me. Aggie will not shut up. She tells so many embarrassing anecdotes from our childhood that it is a relief when the coffee shop starts to close.

Dillon and I say goodbye to Aggie, but not before she whispers about us needing to talk in private. I promise her I'll see her the next day, and we leave with hugs all around.

Dillon walks me back to my dorm building.

"We could just go back to my apartment," he says, looking down at me with a half-smile. I swear he knows just how much that look really gets to me.

"I want to," I say. "But I have a lot to do."

"I understand. I've been falling behind on my work too. You're so distracting." He leans in for a kiss. I wish I could just lose myself in it. How amazing it would be to focus on him, on his lips and his body, without worrying about my massive gambling debt and the gangsters who threatened my twin.

Dillon leaves, and I just want to go inside and curl up on my bed. But I see the glint of headlights in the parking lot across the lawn. When they go off, I see that it's that same tan car.

How dare they threaten Aggie? My Aggie, the only person in this world I love more than myself. Before I can change my mind, I march across the rain-soaked lawn.

The driver's-side window slides down. I expect to see a couple of gangster types. Instead I come face-to-face with a young woman. I'm starting to think I've gone insane. I've mistaken a poor college student for a stalker.

Then she speaks. "Hello, Ester," she says. "I'm Detective Crowley."

Oh shit.

"Get in," she says.

I hesitate.

"Hurry up before my cover is well and truly blown," she says, irritated.

"But I don't understand."

"Your name is Ester Tomasi, you've got a terrible gambling problem, and you're in debt to a crime family. Sound about right?"

I nod.

"Okay, now get in." She holds up her badge. "Or we can do this at the station."

I walk around to the other side of the car. The lock shifts open, and I get in. It's warm inside, and even though it looks like a beater car, it still smells new.

Detective Crowley turns to me. "You okay?"

"Not really." I have so many questions.

"I know," she says. "How am I old enough to be a cop? I have a young face. I got this detail because I can pass for a college student. We tend to focus on drugs and prostitution here on campus, but we know all about the gambling ring your friends have going."

"They're not my friends," I say.

"And they're into more than gambling. We think they're supplying a lot of drugs to the region."

"What does that have to do with me?"

"Well, you could talk. We'll protect you."

"I don't know if I can do that," I say. "They could hurt my family."

"I want you to think about it, Ester. We can get you the help you need." She hands me a card. It's blank save for a phone number. "Call anytime."

I get out and hurry back to my dorm. I don't think I can take any more of this. I feel like I'm going to lose my mind. I'm going to have to come clean.

Chapter Eleven

Back in my room I curl up on my bed, feeling low and paranoid. I'm going to call my parents. I will tell them everything. But I can't seem to get up the nerve to make the call. My phone rings. In a true gift from the universe, it's them, Mom and Dad.

I pick up the phone with trembling fingers. "Hello?"

"Hi there, favorite twin," says Dad. I can hear Mom in the background, chattering at him. "Hang on," he says to me. "What?" I hear him ask her. He comes back. "Sorry, your mom wants to know if it's lasagna or ziti or both."

"Huh? For what?"

"For dinner. We just spoke with Agatha, and she said she is driving you down tomorrow to spend a couple days of reading break with us."

Reading break. Of course! I had forgotten that we have a week off school. Agatha must have planned this, but at least it doesn't sound like she said anything about my debt. A break could be the best thing. If I leave town now, I could talk to Mom and Dad about the money and have it all sorted out before John Jr.'s deadline. I wouldn't have to deal with Detective Crowley.

"Ester?" Dad says. "You there?"

"Huh? Yeah, I'm here. I'll come," I say.

"But what about the food, Ester? You know if I don't tell your mother something soon, she's going to start yelling."

I laugh. "Both," I say. "Tell Mom to make both."

I hang up, feeling more alive, and then send Dillon a quick text letting him know I'll be away. He sends back a few sad face emojis and a note:

I'll miss you, smarty-pants. Hurry back.

Just when I'm down as low as I can go, something comes along to lift me back up. What are the odds?

Chapter Twelve

Aggie is happy to have me all to herself for a long car ride. She has gone full Agatha. A preplanned playlist of our favorite songs (some punk on there for me), unhealthy road snacks, including packaged jerky and a huge bag of candy, and an irritating assortment of road games.

Normally the games would be a deal-breaker for me, but I'm just so grateful to be alone with her for a while. I've missed our Twin Time™ so much.

There's something a little weird about how she's keeping everything so basic and light. It's not like Aggie to be so nonconfrontational. As she drives, I consider asking her outright. I go for something more subtle.

"Everything okay, Ag?" I ask.

"Hmm? Yeah, why?"

"Nothing." I shrug. "You're just so cheery, I guess."

She laughs. "And that's a bad thing?"

"No, not bad at all."

We drive, and she switches to her downer Swedish electronic playlist. It's putting me to sleep.

"You look tired," she says. "Why don't you get some sleep?"

"You're okay to drive the rest of the way?"

"No worries. We'll be there soon."

I recline my seat and drift off.

When I wake up, we're at a rest stop close to home. I sit up and look out the window. Aggie is sitting on a picnic table, looking down at her phone. I get out of the car and stretch, walking over to her stiffly.

"Ugh," I groan. "Remind me not to catch up on sleep in a Volkswagen again. Bad idea." I stop when I see her face. She's crying.

"Aggie, what's wrong?" My heart starts to pound.

She speaks to me through gritted teeth, and that's when I understand she's not sad. And she's not holding her phone. She's holding *mine*. "When were you going to tell me?"

"I-I..." I stammer. I don't know what she knows.

Aggie holds up my phone. "You're way overdrawn in all your accounts. And all these gambling apps and profiles..." She trails off. "I was worried you were on drugs, Ester. And so was Dillon."

I bristle at the mention of his name. "What do you mean?"

She cocks her head at me. "Come on, Ester. We talked, and we both agree something is off."

Wait, *what*? "You mean you talked to *my* boyfriend about me?!" I yell. A few people at the picnic area glance over.

"Calm down."

"No! What right do you have to go through my phone? To violate my privacy like that? And to talk to my boyfriend behind my back? I mean, I knew you were jealous, Agatha, but I didn't think you were desperate."

My words hang in the air between us. Half of me wishes I could undo them, when I note the flash of hurt that crosses her face. The other half of me relishes this. Why does she get to judge me? Why is she trying to ruin the only good thing I have in my life?

Aggie narrows her eyes at me, equally pissed. "I'm telling."

"Go ahead, Agatha. Tattle to Mom and Dad. Then you can be the better twin. It's the only thing you have going for you anyway."

Aggie's lip trembles. She doesn't say anything for several moments. Then she sniffs, straightening up. "No. You can figure this out on your own. I'm done."

By the time we get there, we're both like statues. Mom and Dad notice immediately that something is wrong.

"What happened?" Mom asks as she answers the door. The smell of her cooking wafts out. I fight not to cry.

"Nothing," Aggie mutters.

"Just tired," I say. That part is true. I feel like I could sleep for a decade. Maybe forever.

"Come in, come in," Dad says, ushering us through the door. "We have lots of food. Get you fattened up again," he says, pinching my cheek. "So thin, Ester." He looks me over with concern.

"I'm fine, Dad," I say.

Aggie lets out a snort. "Yeah, right," she mutters under her breath.

I shoot her a deadly look.

Mom looks back and forth between us and clucks her tongue. "I don't like this attitude," she says. "Go wash up, and we'll eat."

Aggie and I always shared a room, and Mom and Dad have kept it the same. Whenever we come back home, it's like no time has passed.

I plop down onto my bed, tossing my backpack on the floor. As I lay back, I wonder if there'll ever be a bed as comfortable as the one you grew up with.

Aggie walks in, sits on her bed and, in her mind-reading way, says, "The thing I really miss is this bed." She lays back too, and we stay there in silence until Dad hollers at us to come to the table.

They have made enough food to last until the end of days. In addition to starters of salad and squid, there's a fifty-layer lasagna, three-cheese ziti, meatballs with Italian gravy, cannelloni, spaghetti with basil, mezzaluna (little half-moon pastas stuffed with seafood), sliced beef in a gorgonzola sauce, and a ton of homemade bread. Not to mention the spread of desserts and cheeses that Mom has set out on the sideboard.

We dig in, eating slowly so as not to fill up too fast, pausing to murmur our gratitude at the delicious feast. When we're done, Dad makes us espresso, and we chat about things going on in the neighborhood.

Free from the immediate threat of the gangsters and the police, I feel a bit more relaxed. Everything is kind of okay until Mom pulls out the cards.

"Who's up for a game of cribbage?" she asks. "Winners get the last piece of pie, losers do the dishes!"

Family game night is a tradition in our home. But just looking at the cards sends me into a cold sweat.

Aggie looks at me sharply. "Es?" she asks. "You okay?"

I feel like I'm in a fishbowl. Everyone is staring at me, and they seem both too close to me and miles away. I can't breathe.

"Ester?" Dad asks, frowning.

I push away from the table, stumbling backward, and almost fall.

"Honey!" Mom steps toward me, but I hold my arms out.

"Don't," I say, my voice strangled. "I don't feel well."

Mom and Dad exchange a look. They're going to find out.

Aggie clears her throat. "There's something going around on campus," she says.

Mom titters and frets.

"It's not serious," Aggie says, coming over to me. "She's just tired."

"Oh, baby," Mom says. "Go ahead and get some sleep."

"I'll come with and get you settled," says Aggie.

I nod, understanding that my sister has saved me. Again.

We both go upstairs to our room, and I lie down. The room is spinning. Maybe I really am sick.

Aggie shuts the door and kneels down next to me.

I can't look at her eyes. It hurts too much. "Please," I whisper. "Don't."

"Es, look at you," she says. "You're skin and bones. You look like a zombie. When is the last time you slept the whole night? I should really take you to the hospital."

"No! You can't," I protest. "They'll find me there."

Aggie looks confused. "Who? Who will find you? Essie, you're scaring me."

I try to wave her off, but she grabs my hand.

"Ester Tomasi, tell me what is wrong—right now."

"I can't, Aggie."

"Es. I'm invoking Twin Truth™."

"No. That doesn't work. We're not kids anymore. This is serious."

Aggie sighs. "Then let's be serious." She looks at me, right into me. "Essie, you're my other half. You can tell me anything."

"I can't." I finally look up into her eyes, at the same shade of brown as mine. But hers are so much softer. Sometime I feel like a photocopy of a person. She's the original, and I pale in comparison.

"Why not?" she asks.

"Because"—I let out a sob—"you won't love me anymore when you find out."

She recoils as if I've struck her but then gets up onto the bed and lies alongside me, wrapping her arms all the way around me.

"That would never happen," she says. Her voice is quiet, certain. "There is a zero percent probability that that could ever occur."

She holds me as I cry.

I tell her my story, at first downplaying how much I owe, then coming clean.

If I thought I was low before, this is lower.

"I love you," she says when I'm finished. "And I'll help you."

"But Mom and Dad..."

"They don't have to know just yet. I have a plan."

"What?"

"We'll sell the car first. Then I'll see how much money I can take out of my savings account."

I nod. "Okay."

"But," she says, "I pay for everything directly now, understand?"

"Yeah," I say. "I think that's for the best."

"And Ester, once this is over, you're going to tell Mom and Dad about your problem yourself. Okay?"

I sniff. "Okay."

We lie there like that for a long time. And for the first time in a long time, I actually feel safe. Maybe everything will work out all right after all. I drift off to sleep and dream about cards and numbers and Aggie's worried eyes.

Chapter Thirteen

When I wake up, Aggie is gone. I stumble downstairs and fling open the front door. The car is gone too. I hope she's gone to get us some breakfast donuts.

"Morning, honey," Mom calls from the kitchen. "Feeling better?"

"Sort of," I say as I wander in, rubbing sleep from my eyes. I'm still so tired, but the scent of Mom's homemade cinnamon waffles perks me up.

Dad shuffles in, wearing his ancient slippers. "Waffles!" he exclaims. "Whoa," he says when he sees me. "You look like you could use some." He sits down at the kitchen island and pulls out a stool for me.

I slide in next to him. "Thanks, Dad."

"Eat," he says, loading up a plate with waffles and placing it in front of me "Eat."

My stomach growls. I take a bite and look up to see both of my parents watching me.

"Well?" Mom says, a cautious smile on her face. I know what she's expecting me to say.

I break into a grin. "These waffles are so good you could get your own cooking show!"

"Better than that Martha Stewart?" Dad asks.

"Martha Stewart wishes she could make a waffle this good," I declare.

They both laugh. It's the same joke we've been making for years.

"Hey, where's Aggie?" I ask. "These are her favorite."

"Oh, I know." Mom sighs. "I sent some along with her for the drive back."

I nearly choke on the chunk of waffle in my throat.

"Back?" I ask. My voice is at least an octave higher.

"Yep," Dad says absently, opening his paper. He's the only person I know who still reads a newspaper cover to cover. "Work called her in. Something about a broken espresso machine."

Mom clucks her tongue. "I don't know why she takes that job so seriously. It's just a coffee shop. And she's going to be a lawyer someday!"

"Now, honey," Dad says, giving Mom a charming smile. "Our girl has a good work ethic. Knows the value of an honest dollar. Isn't that right, Ester?"

I nod. "Yeah," I manage, but it stings. Agatha is the honest one. And I'm not. "But couldn't she have waited for me?"

"Oh, she didn't want to wake you since you weren't feeling well," says Mom.

"We'll give you a ride back tomorrow," Dad says. "Give us a chance to come check up on you both." He winks at me.

Goddamn you, Agatha. This better not be part of her grand plan. Just thinking about it makes me feel sick. I push my plate away.

"Ester, if you're done, maybe you should go back to bed," Mom says. "You look a little green."

"Yeah, honey, get some rest," Dad says. "Mom will bring you some of her special soup later, won't you, hon?"

Mom smiles. "You bet I will."

"And it will certainly be better than Martha What's-her-name's." Dad flashes Mom another cheeky grin. Mom bats her eyelashes.

I almost barf from the cuteness.

Not really. If I manage to get through the next few days alive, and if I ever get old and get married, I hope I have something special like my parents have. Gross as it is sometimes, these two are totally Goals.

"On that note," I say, "I'm going back to bed."

I head upstairs and snuggle up in my bed. Before I go to sleep, I send Aggie some texts:

Where are you really?
Is everything ok?
I'm worried.

She doesn't respond, and the texts don't look like they've been read yet.

I dial Dillon's number, but there's no answer. It goes to voice mail. I realize I have no idea what he's doing for reading break. In fact, I haven't asked him much about his family. I hate leaving voice mails, but I want him to know that I do actually care.

"Hey you," I say, trying to make my voice sound light. "Um, just wanted to say hi and see how your break is going. I should have brought you with me, because there's so many leftovers, we could probably survive the apocalypse. Anyway. I was just missing you. And I wanted you to know that I'm sorry. For being weird. I know you talked to Aggie. And I know you were worried. But it's okay. I'm okay. That's all. I'm coming back tomorrow. Okay, bye."

I hang up, feeling all kinds of nervous and awkward. I can't wait to see him again.

Chapter Fourteen

The drive home is agony. Dad yammers on about how inferior the newfangled electric cars are to the regular kind and Mom insists on listening to a podcast about murderers. Right now I can't stomach stories of violent criminals hunting people down. It's too real. I put in my earbuds.

I text Aggie again. No response. I'm starting to get worried. Dillon got back to me right away with an adorable selfie of him lying in bed with rumpled hair and no shirt. The caption made my heart pound: *Wish you were here.*

When we get to the dorm, Mom and Dad insist on coming up to my room with me. I'm stalling, trying to find a way to tell them I had to sell my stuff, including my Machine. It turns out that this is the least of my worries. As we approach my doorway, I see that Detective Crowley is waiting for me.

"Hello, Ester. We need to talk."

"A friend of yours?" Mom asks.

In this light, the detective looks a lot older than she did the night we talked in her car. More like a cop. To hit that home, she flashes her badge right in my parents' faces.

I feel a surge of hot panic.

"What's going on?" Dad asks. Then his face begins to crack. "Oh god! Agatha!"

Detective Crowley puts up her hands. "Agatha is

fine, Mr. Tomasi. She is safe. She is not hurt. But we have a problem."

"What problem?" Dad demands.

Mom lets out a sigh that sounds more like a whimper. I have never hated myself more.

"Let's go inside and talk," says Detective Crowley. "If that's okay with Ester."

Everyone turns and looks at me.

"Yes," I sigh. I guess it's just time for this.

We crowd inside my tiny dorm room. Both of my parents sit on my bed. They look impossibly small, and young, and I have this weird sense that I'm looking at them for the first time ever. I plunk down in my office chair. Mom and Dad are too worried to notice the missing computer.

Detective Crowley leans against the windowsill. She peeks out between the blinds for a moment. "Look, time is of the essence," she says. "Ester, I'm assuming your parents don't have any idea what this is about?"

I nod, and both of my parents swivel their heads at me.

"Okay. I'll get this over with. Mr. and Mrs. Tomasi, I'm very sorry to inform you that your daughter has a serious gambling problem. She is in significant debt to individuals who are involved in gang activity."

Mom starts crying. "But that doesn't sound like Agatha at all."

Dad frowns and looks at me. He knows the truth.

"No, Mom," I say. "It's me. I'm the one with the problem." It feels like I'm carving the words out from my chest.

"I'm sure you have questions, concerns," Detective Crowley says to my parents. "But we need to address the fact that we arrested your other daughter today on drug-trafficking charges."

Now it's my turn to be shocked. "*What?*"

"Well," Detective Crowley says, "it looks like Agatha decided to visit the club, perhaps to clear your debt."

Of course she did.

"She went into the club, and our team was very concerned. You see, they thought she was you. They thought you might end up getting hurt."

"Oh my god, no!" Mom cries. "This isn't happening."

"So when Agatha did come out, our team moved on her to take her in. For her—your—protection." The detective looks at me. "Honestly, it almost screwed up the whole investigation. We didn't want to go in that early and show our hand, so we waited until she came back out of the club. We thought we might find some contraband on her to make a charge, but she actually had a significant amount of illegal drugs on her person."

When she says this last part, we all stare at her, mouths open.

Detective Crowley nods. "Apparently, she agreed to work for them selling narcotics and said she'd convince you to work for them too. She promised them that the pair of you could sell way more on campus to your peers than they could at the club or on the street. But, of course, her plan all along had been to come to the police. We just happened to have intercepted her. It doesn't look good on paper, but I think we can make a case with a judge to get it taken care of."

"You have to!" I shout. Detective Crowley narrows her eyes at me, and I force myself to lower my voice. "I only mean she did it for me. Agatha is pre-law. She's squeaky clean."

"I know," Detective Crowley says. "Now get your things, and let's go."

"Where?" we all ask at once.

"To make it right."

Chapter Fifteen

I take a minute to gather my things, avoiding my parents' gaze. There is a knock at the door.

"Can I get that?" I ask.

Detective Crowley looks through the peephole. She sighs. "Just your boyfriend."

What a shitstorm.

Dad clears his throat. "Make it quick, Ester."

As I slip out the door, Detective Crowley grabs my elbow. "I have people outside," she warns.

I shut the door behind me. Wow, no one trusts me. Why would they?

Dillon is leaning against the wall, all tall, dark and sexy. I take a moment to drink him in.

"What?" he asks. "Your face is weird."

"Yeah," I say. "Because after I tell you what I have to tell you, I'm pretty sure this is the last time I'll see you. And I want to remember this."

"What do you mean?" He comes over to me, concern all over his beautiful face. "Did you fall in love with another gentleman caller?"

"Stop. This is serious."

"Okay," he says quietly. "I'm listening."

I have to be quick, so I spill it all to him in a big gush of words. He listens as I finish the whole sordid tale.

"I understand if you want to walk away and never talk to me again," I say at last.

"No," he says after a moment. "I don't want to do that. I care about you, Essie."

My hand finds my lucky coin in my pocket, and I pull it out, flipping it over and over in my fingers.

"Have you ever thought of selling that thing?" he asks. "It doesn't seem that lucky."

"My grandfather gave it to me. And besides, I don't think it's worth much."

"Well, you never know. I read an article a while back about common coins that are actually valuable. I searched through all my loose change, and I had nothing good. But who knows? Might be worth checking out."

Come to think of it, that pawnshop guy was kind of interested. I have an idea.

"Maybe you could help me?" I ask.

"Sure, babe. Anything."

I hand over the coin, my hand shaking. "If you can sell it, do. And give the money to my dad." I have

been kidding myself about its sentimental value.
I need to start making some changes.

"And if it's worthless?" he asks.

"Throw it off a goddamned bridge or something."

He leans in to give me a sweet kiss on the forehead. "I'll toss it off the highest bridge I can find, babe."

Chapter Sixteen

At the police station, I wait in an interview room while Mom and Dad process Aggie's release. After a while my parents come back, along with Detective Crowley and a very tired-looking lawyer named Ms. Scott.

Dad's anger is still palpable. "Ester, let's talk," he says.

Everyone sits around a conference table and listens while I tell my story. Ms. Scott records everything and takes notes (after advising me that I don't have to talk at all). It feels better to get it all out in the open. Besides, the truth will set Agatha free. Literally. My parents listen, bewildered.

Once I'm done, Ms. Scott thanks me. "I think I have enough to convince my boss not to lay charges against Agatha," she says. "But there are going to be some conditions."

"Such as?" Dad asks.

"Ester is going to have to commit to cooperating with the police on this investigation, and she'll have to agree to counseling. In-patient rehab. Ninety-day minimum."

"That's okay," I say. "I'll do anything to help Agatha."

"Good," says Ms. Scott. "Detective?"

"Thank you. Here's what's going to happen next," says Detective Crowley. "Agatha will be set free once a judge signs off, but she will need to stay in the area. She will even have to go to classes. It needs to seem like everything is normal."

"And me?" I ask.

"You'll work with us on our sting to take down the drug and gambling ring. Once our operation is done, you'll head off to rehab."

"You mean to tell me that you're planning to put my child in harm's way?" Dad is barely holding it together.

"Yes," Detective Crowley says. "Let's face it. She was already doing a good job of that all on her own." She sighs. "Look, it sounds worse than it is. Ester will be safe. We just need her to make a buy from her contacts at the club so we can get it on tape. That's all. Ester can do this. She's been there before."

"Dad," I say. "I can do this. For Aggie."

"I don't like it," he says. "What if we say no?"

"Then you roll the dice with the court," says

Ms. Scott. "It sounds harsh, and it is, but that's the deal."

"I'll do it," I say. "Where do I sign?"

After going through all the processing and paperwork, my parents are finally allowed to take me back to a cheap motel just outside of town, where the cops have put us all up.

Mom and Dad had to sign scary documents saying they would not leave me alone, not even for a minute. So it's just me and them and their intense disappointment, trapped in a room while the police set up the sting.

Mom does what she does best—arranging food for us to eat from the nearby diner. Dad and I sit on the ugly beds and watch TV. Dad flips through the channels and lands on *Wheel of Fortune*. Then he quickly clicks it off.

"It's okay," I say. "Pat Sajak's not going to trigger me to gamble."

"This is not a joking matter," he snaps.

I don't reply. He's right.

He takes a deep breath. "I'm sorry," he says. "This is all my fault."

"This is not your fault, Dad!"

"I'm a parent. Of course it's my fault," he says. "And I think you got your addiction from me."

"What are you talking about? You don't gamble."

"No, I don't. I don't drink either," he says. "Because I'm an alcoholic."

What? How have I not known this? "I just thought you didn't like the taste of alcohol."

"Nope," he says. "I love it."

"But..."

"Ester, I have been sober since the day you were born. You know why? I was drunk when your mom went into labor with you two. I was completely useless to her. I wasn't there. I didn't even hold you until you were a few days old."

"I didn't know that."

"Because your mom is a saint," he says.

We sit in silence for a minute, the whir of the motel heating system the only sound.

"I want you to understand that people can do bad things, and make bad choices, but they can come back from it," he says. "I don't want you to use this low point as an excuse to harm yourself even more."

"I guess you do know something about it, huh?" I say, feeling understood for the first time.

"You have to get off this merry-go-round," he says.

"But," I say, "how do you get excited about life then? Aren't you bored all the time?"

"Bored? You mean with my comfortable life, being alive and having two amazing kids and a wife who's a better cook than Martha Stewart?"

I laugh.

"Yeah, real boring," he says.

Mom opens the door and sees us sitting there. Her arms are full of takeout containers. "Let's see how good this diner's chicken parmesan really is, shall we?" she says.

"There's no way it's better than yours, Mom," I say, getting up to take the containers from her.

Not a chance.

Chapter Seventeen

Dillon calls. He's got an update on my coin. I can't tell him where I am, so I arrange for him to drop off a letter to Detective Crowley at the station. She delivers it when she comes to brief us on the next steps.

I take it to the bathroom to read it. When I open the envelope there is a cashier's check inside for $8,000. Oh my god.

It's made out to Ralph Tomasi, which is a relief. I nearly pass out from the irony of having had this coin in my pocket the whole time.

Dillon really came through. He could have taken that money for himself and split. Of course, he didn't. He includes a note.

Babe,

Your UNlucky coin wasn't worthless after all! It was a 1970-S Proof Washington quarter, as you know. But it was one of the better-quality ones. One of these suckers sold for almost 40 grand! Sorry yours wasn't quite that good. Turns out that finding one is even more rare than getting hit by lightning. Or, even more rare than that, finding a brown-eyed girl who makes me feel the way you do.

Yeah, I said it.

Be safe,

—D

I walk out of the bathroom, trembling. I hand dad the check.

"What is this?" he asks.

"I sold the quarter Granddad gave me. With Dillon's help."

I show him the note, and he reads it.

"Good," he says at last. "And this is a special guy you've found."

"I guess I can make some good decisions," I say.

Dad sighs and reaches for his wallet. He fishes something out of it. It's a large brass token. He hands it to me.

"What is it?"

"It's the AA coin I got when I decided to get sober."

I look at it. It says, *To Thine Own Self Be True.* I laugh. "*Hamlet* again."

He looks at me, puzzled.

"There's this character in *Hamlet*," I explain. "Polonius. And he's always giving advice to his son. That's one of his lines. 'To thine own self be true.' "

"It's a good one," Dad says.

"Yeah. He also says, 'Neither a borrower nor a lender be.' "

"Hmm. Guess you should have paid more attention in English class, huh?" he asks.

"Yeah, guess so."

"What you do now is what matters," says Mom.

"I hurt people, Mom. You and Dad. And Aggie. No matter what I do in my life, that's the worst thing. When you're a twin, it's like you don't have just one life. You have two."

Mom nods. "You could see that as a burden. Or you could see it as a gift."

Detective Crowley walks back in. "Hate to interrupt, but are you ready to do the hardest thing you've ever done?"

"Yes," I say.

And I am. I will not let Aggie down.

Chapter Eighteen

Aggie has been released, but I can't see her yet. She has to resume her normal routine in case we're being watched. I've got to play the part of a college student with a severe gambling addiction. Not a stretch.

Once the police brief me on my mission—go to the club, try to buy drugs—I'm let loose into the big wide world. I'm "free," only this time I've got a recording device under my clothes and a surveillance crew watching my every move.

Mom and Dad are so worried they can't even eat, which is saying something. But they understand this is what I have to do if Aggie and I have any shot at a future.

So here I am, standing across the road from the club, late at night, while the wind blows through me. All I can think about is the card game that is probably happening just inside those doors. You know that term *triggering*? This is it, times a million.

I have some cash the cops gave me that I'm supposed to give the gangsters as payment. It would be a lot easier without the wire. I'm so paranoid, I can't think straight. It's all coming together for my general look of strung-out chic.

When I knock on the door, it's Big Steve who answers. Relief floods through me. Even though he is creepy, he's not that bright.

"Well, look here," he sneers. "Essssssssssie. I met your sister. She's even cuter than you."

"Yeah," I say. Ugh. So creepy.

"You got the rest of our money?" Big Steve asks.

"Most of it."

"Most?" His eyes narrow.

"Aggie said that I could make up for it. You know, by helping you guys out."

"Where is your double anyway?" asks a voice, and John Jr. steps forward from the darkness. He's been watching and listening. "I haven't seen her around for a couple of days. I'm disappointed."

"Yeah, she's busy. She's going to a bunch of the frat parties this weekend. Big holiday event. Lots of opportunities to move the product."

John Jr. stares at me awhile. "Thought maybe she was going to rat," he says finally.

I shake my head. "No way. Aggie's smart. That's why I'm here."

John Jr. raises an eyebrow.

"She needs more. Says there's way too much demand." The lies are coming easier to me now, and it's just like old times. Talking fast and finding my way in was always my specialty. Who would have thought I'd need those skills for a moment like this?

They stare at me, and it's like time slows down. To keep from panicking, I count the seconds. They study me for eleven seconds before John Jr. nods at Big Steve. He steps aside to let me in. If you think eleven seconds isn't a long time, try having two dangerous guys stare you down for that length of time while you attempt to record them committing a felony. Then tell me how quick it is.

"Back here," John Jr. says, leading the way.

It's just my luck that tonight there's a poker game going on. It's like sensory overload. I take in the bright overhead lights, the haze of cigar smoke, the green felt of the semicircular table, the sound of cards being shuffled and the tin-can electric taste of nerves on my tongue.

Big Steve turns. "What do you say, Essssssie? Want to get in on the action?"

"Nah," says John Jr. "She's cut off, Stevo."

"I don't know, Johnny, she looks ready to up her debt to me..." He trails off.

For once in his stupid life, Big Steve is actually right. I've never wanted to sit down at the poker table more than I do right now. I know that's only because I'm scared and I'm trying to find a way to feel better.

I look at the players at the table. All of them are transfixed by the cards and the chips. Their faces all have the same hypnotized look of devotion. Underneath it, though, I can see their desperation. Everyone in this room is part of the same sickness. And I'm going to end it.

"You know," I say to John Jr., "I think I'm kind of over the poker scene."

"That so?" He cocks his eyebrow at me, not believing me.

"I'm kind of into something else now," I say, remembering that the cops told me they found just under a kilo of narcotics on Aggie. It was molly, the party drug.

"Aggie's supply," I start. "It's light."

"Light?" Big Steve asks.

"Yeah. We can clear that kilo in a weekend. We need to think bigger."

"Bigger?" Big Steve echoes me again.

"I'm listening," says John Jr.

"Molly is done," I say. "I mean, everyone does it, but only once in a while. They don't do it every night."

"Go on," says John Jr.

"Better to give us something we can sell every day. For a bigger return on our investment."

"Such as?" Big Steve asks.

"Some kind of upper that helps you study. Like Ritalin or Adderall."

"We don't do prescriptions," says John Jr. "Too labor-intensive."

"Okay," I say, finally leading them to where I want them. "Then crystal. An intense, short-term high. Super addictive."

I feel disgusting, saying this out loud. I almost forget I'm lying. I would never deal drugs to my fellow students. After all, I wanted to be a doctor before I screwed up my whole life.

I'm terrified they're going to get suspicious and discover the wire, but I keep my cool. I finally understand how my sister must have felt, standing here in this same situation—and for me.

John Jr. and Big Steve talk for a while and then turn to me.

"You sure you two little girls can handle something as heavy as this?" John Jr. asks.

"Of course."

"This isn't a bit of molly. This is harder shit. And tweakers aren't to be trifled with. What are you going to do if one of them tries to rob you?"

I hesitate. "I'll carry a gun," I say. "Or hire some muscle."

John Jr. lets out a loud laugh. "I'd like to see that, kid."

"Look," I say. "You give me a few kilos of crystal to start. I bet I'll be back in two days for double that amount. We can clear a hundred grand in a weekend. I've got skills and a 150 IQ. I think I can manage some protective resources and the necessary tools for the job. Unless, of course, you guys can't handle that kind of action."

That was a bold move. Will it work? Or was I just too cocky?

They stare at me.

Finally John Jr. breaks into a smile. "Take her to the cooler, Stevo."

"With pleasure," Big Steve says. "This way." He grabs me by the elbow and shoves me along in front of him. "Move."

We walk down a back hallway I've never seen before until we come to a set of heavy doors. Refrigerated doors. I can feel bile rising in my throat. I wonder if the police will make it in here quickly enough to save me before Big Steve murders me in a meat cooler.

He reaches out a thick forearm and pulls open the latch. The door swings outward. I'm expecting to see a *GoodFellas*-style scene of frozen gangster bodies hanging from meat hooks. But it's just a cold room filled with cardboard boxes.

"In," Big Steve grunts.

I step inside, hoping he doesn't notice my legs shaking.

John Jr. pushes past me and opens a box. He dumps its contents in front of me—several sealed bags filled with crystalline rocks.

"Wow," I say. "That's some nice-looking meth." God, I hope the police can hear me back here. I swallow, going in for the kill. "You got more? Or is this your whole wad?"

John Jr. chuckles. His ego is his downfall. He pulls a knife, and I'm amazed when I don't flinch. He cuts open several more boxes, all of them filled with drugs.

"That enough for you?" he asks. "You really think you can move all this?"

"Well," I say, pretending to think. "How much exactly do we have here?"

He shrugs. "At least a hundred keys, maybe more."

"Yeah," brags Big Steve. "Our dad has connections. He's got the primo stuff."

"Shut up!" John Jr. spits. "You're not supposed to talk about Dad."

"Right, sorry," says Big Steve.

"So what do you say, kid?" John Jr. asks. "Are we going to get rich or what?"

I smile. "Guess it's your lucky day."

Chapter Nineteen

The police waited until I walked out of there with a backpack and two duffel bags full of meth. They wanted it to look like a random bust instead of a sting. They'd been trying to get something on the owner of the club for a long time. I guess John Jr. and Big Steve were pretty small potatoes. It was their dad the cops were after.

Instead of jail, Detective Crowley takes me directly to the airport. Time for rehab. I'll have to stay there for ninety days, minimum. When I get to the departures gate, my parents are both there, along with a surprise. Aggie is here to see me off. It's the first time we've seen each other since that night at our family home.

When I see her, I fall apart. The pain of everything I've done overwhelms me.

"Aggie," I say through sobs, "I'm so sorry."

"I know," she whispers, squeezing me with one of her great hugs. "I always know, Es. It's Twin Power™, remember?"

I laugh. "Yeah. I guess you could have got yourself a better twin though, huh?"

"No," she says, pushing my bangs back from my eyes. "There is a zero percent probability of that."

"I guess the odds are astronomical."

"Es," she says. "Make me a promise, okay?"

"Of course."

"Be nice to yourself," she says. "You don't have to be perfect. Just be good to you."

I nod. "I have to learn how to do that. I'll try."

Dad, my chaperone for this trip, holds up his wrist, pointing to his watch. It's time to go.

"Ag, can you do something else for me?" I ask, trying not to bawl.

"Anything."

"Will you check in on Dillon while I'm gone?" I ask. "Just, like, make sure he's happy, okay?"

"I will," she says. "Matter of fact, he sent a letter for you." She presses an envelope into my hand.

I grab her into one more hug before I pull away and follow Dad to my uncertain future.

On the plane, I open Dillon's letter. It's exactly what I wanted to see.

Sugar,

I'm proud of you. I miss you. I'll be here when you get back.

Love,

D

Sugar. The word repeats in my mind. It stays with me throughout my hard days and weeks at the rehab center. It's scary here, with all the broken people trying to find their way again. I'm learning a lot about myself, about why I do the things I do and how I can build a future.

Aggie emails every day, updating me on Dillon (doing great, still hot), and school (she's getting all A's, of course). She tells me John Jr. and Big Steve turned on each other, sold each other out. Imagine that. Brothers!

In their phone calls, Mom and Dad assure me that Aggie is safe, but I worry. I always worry. I'll never forgive myself for putting her in danger, even though she has forgiven me.

I think I'm going to stay out here for a while, where it's warm and I'm away from my old habits. It's so hard being away from Aggie, but it's for the best. We'll still have Twin Time™ on Skype, and no matter how far away she is, we'll always be as close as two human beings can be.

As for Dillon, he's almost done his undergrad, and he's thinking about where he wants to go next. In his emails he tells me there's a certain sweetheart of his in sunny climes that he may have to call upon. Or some kind of old-timey nonsense talk like that.

My parents are wonderful. They decided to downsize a little and bought an RV, so now they can go back and forth between me and Aggie. Mom is happy to be able to deliver ziti and lasagna. Dad is happy when Mom is happy, so everybody wins.

I don't think I'm going to graduate with Aggie. I don't think I'll be some hot-shot pre-med kid genius anymore. I see a new future for myself, maybe in counseling.

Every day I get to make my own decisions and stand by them, and I get to live by the advice of old Polonius: *To thine own self be true.* I get to be me, and there's a high probability that I am not perfect. Like Hamlet, I've suffered the slings and arrows of outrageous fortune, and I've come out the other side. It's going to be okay, I think. This is my life. Win, lose or draw.

Acknowledgments

I am eternally grateful to the entire team at Orca Book Publishers for the opportunity to make books with them. You do incredible work. Thank you to my teachers for sharing great literature with me, and for making Shakespeare such an important part of my life. I'd also like to thank Tom Stoppard for writing a brilliant play and one of my favorite movies of all time. As always, I am so thankful for my family's support, love, and endless, endless chances.

LOGAN USES HER CAMERA TO WORK THROUGH THE LOSS OF HER MOM.

"Tackles serious topics with sincerity."
—*Kirkus Reviews*

WILL JOINING A PUNK BAND HELP KALLIE FIND HER PURPOSE?

"A thoroughly modern and realistic love story."
—*Resource Links*

orca soundings

Star Spider

HEY JUDE

Penny is busy enough with school and taking care of her sister. She doesn't have time for love, but then she meets Jack.

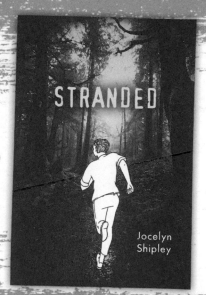

STRANDED

Jocelyn Shipley

Could Kipp's lucky break of landing a job and a place to live be too good to be true?

Brooke Carter is the author of several contemporary books for teens, including *Learning Seventeen* and *The Unbroken Hearts Club* from the Orca Soundings line, and the YA fantasy series Runecaster.

orca soundings

For more information on all the books
in the Orca Soundings line, please visit
orcabook.com.